THE MIDNIGHT CLUB

Written by SHANE GOTH

Illustrated by YONG LING KANG

OWLKIDS BOOKS

WHILE HER FAMILY SLEPT,
Milly lay awake, waiting.

At exactly midnight, she woke her big sister.

Becca held up a finger on one hand and two on the other. Milly did the same. The sign of the Midnight Club.

Darkness tingled on Milly's skin. She'd never
been up so late.
Becca slowly opened the door. "Let's go."

They stopped outside their parents' room.

Milly's heart went *ba-dum thump.*

Becca slinked. Milly stepped.

They smiled when they got past.

Shadows crisscrossed the hall.

"Tiptoe over each one," Becca whispered.

Milly gulped. "I can't touch any?"

"It's a rule of the Midnight Club."

Becca hopped.

Milly leaped…
and wobbled.

"Just one more big step,"
Becca said.

Milly **streeeeeetched** her leg.

The stairs were old and creaky. Becca sneaked.

Milly creeped. A stair squeaked.

"Shhhhh," said Becca.

Milly held her breath. The house stayed quiet.

Milly had never been downstairs in the middle of the night. The walls were blue with moonlight. It looked like their own secret planet.

Becca got comfy in Dad's chair.

"He never lets us sit there," Milly said.

"Another rule of the Midnight Club: do whatever you want." Becca opened Dad's jar of jelly beans and ate a handful.

Milly took a few, too. "My favorite's blue!"

Milly pulled down Mom's raincoat. "Try this on."

Becca did. "Do I look like Mom?"

"Not even close," Milly teased.

Becca scowled and chased her.

The ceiling creaked. Footsteps!

Milly hugged her sister and they hid under the
coat until the house was quiet once more.

Milly peeked out and spotted a
dark shape on the wall. A big head
and sharp teeth.

"A monster!"

"It's just the streetlight making shadows," Becca said.

They held things up in the light and created new monsters.

"This one's Scarf-enstein."

"Here's Count Plant-ula."

They giggled and made their monsters dance.

A scratch at the back door. Milly
jumped behind Becca. Her heart went
boom bump boom.

Becca said, "It's the President of the Midnight
Club." She let in Oliver, their cat.
Milly tickled under his chin. "Yep, we're up, too."
But her eyes felt heavy.

"What should we do, President Oliver?"
Becca asked.

He dashed under the table. So did
Becca and Milly. Oliver pounced on a chair
and licked water from a bowl. They did, too.
He jumped up on the couch.

Milly stretched.

"You're tired, aren't you?" Becca said.

"Am not!"

Becca yawned. "Fine, we can stop for tonight.
Since *you* want to." She started up the stairs.

"Wait!" said Milly. "You forgot the most
important rule of the Midnight Club: we have to
keep it a secret." She put back Dad's jelly beans,
munching on a few more blue ones, and hung
up Mom's coat.

"Follow me." Milly sneaked.

She creeped and leaped.

Becca and Oliver did the same.

All three members of the Midnight Club cuddled together in Milly's bed. Becca sighed. Oliver purred.

"Can we do this again tomorrow night?" Milly whispered.

But Becca was already sleeping. Milly snuggled close with her big sister, the secret of the Midnight Club safe inside her.

To Addie, Eliza, and Claire,
for staying up late with me — S.G.

To my adorable nieces! — Y.L.K.